D0842192

This book belongs to:

....

....

Retold by Monica Hughes
Illustrated by Adrienne Salgado

Reading consultants: Betty Root and Monica Hughes

Marks and Spencer p.l.c.
PO Box 3339
Chester, CH99 9QS

shop online
www.marksandspencer.com

ISBN 978-1-84461-857-6
Printed in China

First Readers

Read Together

Little Red
Riding Hood

**MARKS &
SPENCER**

Helping your child to read

First Readers are closely linked to the National Curriculum. Their vocabulary has been carefully selected from the word lists recommended by the National Literacy Strategy.

Read the story
Read the story
to your child
a few times.

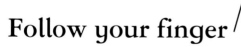

Little Red Riding Hood saw some flowers in the woods.
"I will pick some flowers for Granny," she said.
Little Red Riding Hood stopped to pick the flowers.
Then she met a wolf.

12

Follow your finger
Run your finger under
the text as you read.
Your child will soon begin to
follow the words with you.

Look at the pictures

Talk about the pictures. They will help your child to understand the story.

She met a wolf.

13

Have a go

Let your child have a go at reading the large type on each right-hand page. It repeats a line from the story.

Join in

When your child is ready, encourage them to join in with the main story text. Shared reading is the first step to reading alone.

Once there was a little girl called
Little Red Riding Hood.

One day her mother said,
"Granny is ill.
Please go and see her.
You can take her this basket of fruit."

Little Red Riding Hood.

Granny lived in a house in the woods.
So Little Red Riding Hood took the
basket of fruit.
And she went into the woods to see
her granny.

She went into the woods to
see her granny.

Little Red Riding Hood saw some
flowers in the woods.
"I will pick some flowers for
Granny," she said.
Little Red Riding Hood stopped to
pick the flowers.
Then she met a wolf.

She met a wolf.

The wolf was hungry.
He wanted to eat Little Red
Riding Hood.
"What are you doing in the
woods?" he said sweetly.
Little Red Riding Hood said,
"I'm going to see my granny.
She lives in a house in the woods."

"I'm going to see my granny."

The bad wolf said to himself, "I will go
to Granny's house and eat her."
So the wolf ran to Granny's house.

When the wolf got to Granny's house
he ate her in one gulp.
The wolf put on Granny's clothes and
got into her bed.

The wolf put on Granny's
clothes.

Little Red Riding Hood got to
Granny's house.
She knocked on the door.
"Come in, come in," said the wolf.
"Hello!" said Little Red Riding Hood.

"Hello!" said Little
Red Riding Hood.

Little Red Riding Hood went up to
the bed.

"What big eyes you have!" she said.
So the wolf said sweetly,
"All the better to see you with."

"But what big ears you have!" she said.
So the wolf said very sweetly,
"All the better to hear you with!"

"What big eyes you have!"

Then Little Red Riding Hood said,
"Yes, but what big teeth you have!"
And the wolf said very, very sweetly,
"All the better to eat you with."

And then the wolf jumped out of bed.

"What big teeth you have!"

"I'm going to eat you!" said the wolf.
So Little Red Riding Hood cried,
"Help! Help!"
But the wolf ate her in one gulp.

"I'm going to eat you!" said
the wolf.

A woodcutter was in the woods.
He heard Little Red Riding Hood.
So the woodcutter ran to help.

The woodcutter killed the wolf.
He cut the wolf open.
Granny and Little Red Riding Hood
jumped out.
They were very happy.

Granny and Little Red Riding
Hood jumped out.

Look back in your book.

Can you read these words?

Granny

wolf

basket

house

bed

flowers

Can you answer these questions?

Where did
Granny live?

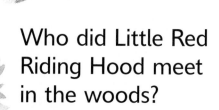

Who did Little Red
Riding Hood meet
in the woods?

Who killed the wolf?

First Readers

(subject to availability)

Beauty and the Beast
Cinderella
The Elves and the Shoemaker
The Emperor's New Clothes
The Enormous Turnip
The Gingerbread Man
Goldilocks and the Three Bears
Hansel and Gretel
Jack and the Beanstalk
Little Red Riding Hood
The Princess and the Pea
Rapunzel
Rumpelstiltskin
Sleeping Beauty
Snow White and the Seven Dwarfs
The Three Billy Goats Gruff
The Three Little Pigs
The Ugly Duckling